# DISNEY's

## A Winnie the Pooh First Reader

# Pooh Gets Stuck

ADAPTED BY Isabel Gaines

ILLUSTRATED BY Nancy Stevenson

DISNEY
PRESS

NEW YORK

# Pooh
# Gets Stuck

Winnie the Pooh was hungry.

Hungry for honey!

Now, honey rhymes with bunny.

And bunny means rabbit . . .

So Pooh set off to visit
his good friend Rabbit.
Rabbit always had honey
at his house.

"Come in, Pooh," said Rabbit.

"You're just in time for lunch."

That's just what Pooh

was hoping to hear.

He squeezed in through

Rabbit's front door.

Pooh sat down

at the table

and began to eat.

Pooh ate and ate.

And then he ate some more.

At last, Pooh stood up

and patted his tummy.

"I must be going now," he said

in a rather sticky voice.

"Good-bye, Rabbit."

Pooh started out the door . . .

And then he stopped!

Pooh's head was already outside.

But his feet were still inside.

His big, round tummy

was stuck in the middle.

Rabbit gave Pooh a push.

Rabbit gave Pooh a poke.

Nothing seemed to help.

Pooh stayed where he was.

"There is only one thing to do,"

Rabbit said.

And off he went to find

Christopher Robin.

11

Pooh waited for Rabbit to return.

He waited and waited.

Finally, Rabbit came back

with Christopher Robin.

Christopher Robin

patted Pooh's head.

"Silly old bear," he said.

Christopher Robin took hold
of Pooh's paw.
Rabbit took hold
of Christopher Robin's shirt.
Then they pulled
as hard as they could.
But poor Pooh stayed stuck.

"There's only one thing to do,"

Christopher Robin told Pooh.

"We must wait for you

to get thin again.

Thin enough to slip

through Rabbit's door."

So Pooh and the others waited.

After a while Eeyore came by.

He looked at Pooh and sighed.

"This could take days,"

Eeyore said.

"Or weeks," he went on.

"Or maybe even months."

"Oh, bother," said Pooh.

"Oh, bother," Rabbit agreed.

Pooh soon got tired of waiting.

Pooh was not happy.

He was hungry!

He got hungrier and hungrier

each day.

That night Gopher popped up

outside Rabbit's hole.

He opened up a big lunch box.

"Time for my midnight snack,"

Gopher told Pooh.

"Snack?" Pooh said hungrily.

19

Inside, Rabbit heard voices.

He jumped out of bed.

Rabbit did not want

Pooh snacking.

He wanted Pooh thin!

He wanted Pooh gone!

Rabbit ran out the backdoor.

Just in time.

Gopher was about to give Pooh

some honey.

"No, no, no!" Rabbit cried.

"Not one drop!"

Rabbit grabbed the honeypot.

Then he made a sign

and stuck it in the ground.

The sign read:

DO NOT FEED THE BEAR

23

Days passed.

Nights passed.

Pooh was still stuck.

Then one day, it happened.

Rabbit leaned against Pooh,

and Pooh moved.

But just a bit.

Rabbit raced off

to get some help.

Rabbit returned with Eeyore,

Kanga, Roo, and

Christopher Robin.

Christopher Robin grabbed

Pooh's paws.

Kanga grabbed Christopher Robin.

Eeyore grabbed Kanga.

Roo grabbed Eeyore.

Rabbit ran inside

and pushed Pooh's legs.

The others pulled his paws.

Push!

Pull!

Push!

Pop!

Pooh flew out of the doorway

and crashed into a hollow tree.

A honey tree!

Eeyore looked up at the tree.

Pooh's legs were waving

in the breeze.

"Stuck again," Eeyore sighed.

"Don't worry,"
Christopher Robin
called up to Pooh.
"We'll get you right out."

But Pooh was in no hurry.

There was honey above him.

Honey below him.

Honey all around him.

"Take your time,

Christopher Robin,"

Pooh called down.

"Take your time!"

# Collect all your favorites from this Brand New Pooh Series!

**Available now**

## POOH GETS STUCK
Tr. ed. 0-7868-4184-2  $3.95 ($5.50)

## POOH'S HONEY TREE
Tr. ed. 0-7868-4253-9  $3.95 ($5.50)

**Available October**

## POOH'S PUMPKIN
Tr. ed. 0-7868-4256-3  $3.95 ($5.50)

## RABBIT GETS LOST
Tr. ed. 0-7868-4254-7  $3.95 ($5.50)

**Available December**

## BOUNCE, TIGGER, BOUNCE
Tr. ed. 0-7868-4255-5  $3.95 ($5.50)

## HAPPY BIRTHDAY, EEYORE
Tr. ed. 0-7868-4183-4  $3.95 ($5.50)

# READ ALL THE DISNEY FIRST READERS

**ARIEL'S TREASURE HUNT**
Level 1
Pbk. ed. 0-7868-4167-2
$2.95 ($3.95)

**RUN, GUS, RUN!**
Level 1
Pbk. ed. 0-7868-4169-9
$2.95 ($3.95)

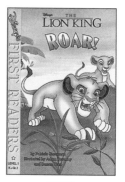

**ROAR!**
Level 1
Pbk. ed. 0-7868-4076-5
$2.95 ($3.95)

**WHERE'S FLIT?**
Level 1
Pbk. ed. 0-7868-4075-7
$2.95 ($3.95)

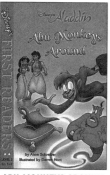

**ABU MONKEYS AROUND**
Level 2
Pbk. ed. 0-7868-4071-4
$2.95 ($3.95)

**THE BEAST'S FEAST**
Level 2
Pbk. ed. 0-7868-4072-2
$2.95 ($3.95)

**HIDE-AND-SEEK**
Level 2
Pbk. ed. 0-7868-4074-9
$2.95 ($3.95)

**PUPPY PARADE**
Level 2
Pbk. ed. 0-7868-4170-2
$2.95 ($3.95)

**BUZZ AND THE BUBBLE PLANET**
Level 3
Pbk. ed. 0-7868-4168-0
$3.50 ($4.95)

**GENIE SCHOOL**
Level 3
Pbk. ed. 0-7868-4073-0
$3.50 ($4.95)

**HERCULES AND THE MAZE OF THE MINOTAUR**
Level 3
Pbk. ed. 0-7868-4171-0
$3.50 ($4.95)

**PARADE DAY**
Level 3
Pbk. ed. 0-7868-4106-0
$3.50 ($4.95)

# Enjoy the Many Tales
# of the Most Beloved of Bears
# in One Beautiful Treasury!

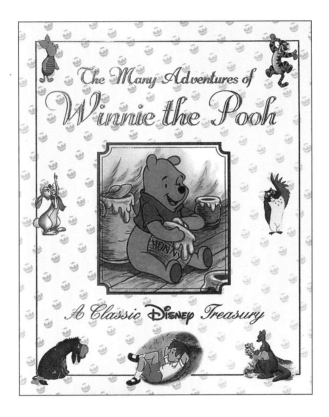

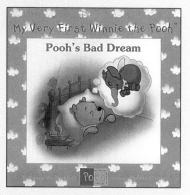

**POOH'S BAD DREAM**
Tr. ed. 0-7868-3137-5   $11.95 ($15.95)

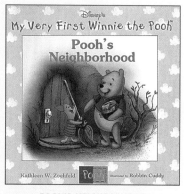

**POOH'S NEIGHBORHOOD**
Tr. ed. 0-7868-3136-7   $11.95 ($15.95)

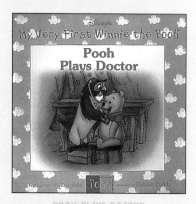

**POOH PLAYS DOCTOR**
Tr. ed. 0-7868-3124-3   $11.95 ($15.95)

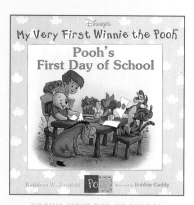

**POOH'S FIRST DAY OF SCHOOL**
Tr. ed. 0-7868-3125-1   $11.95 ($15.95)

**POOH'S WELCOMES WINTER**
Tr. ed. 0-7868-3146-4   $11.95 ($15.95)

**HAPPY NEW YEAR, POOH!**
Tr. ed. 0-7868-3144-8   $11.95 ($15.95)

# oin the Pooh Friendship Club!

A wonder-filled year of friendly activities and interactive fun for your child!

## he fun starts with:

Clubhouse play kit
Exclusive club T-shirt
The first issue of "Pooh News"
Toys, stickers and gifts
from Pooh

## The fun goes on with:

- Quarterly issues of "Pooh News" each with special surprises
- Birthday and Friendship Day cards from Pooh
- And more!

Join now and also get a colorful, collectible Pooh art print

Yearly membership costs just $25 plus 15 Hunny Pot Points. (Look for Hunny Pot Points 3 on Pooh products.)

To join, send check or money order and Hunny Pot Points to:

Pooh Friendship Club
P.O. Box 1723
Minneapolis, MN 55440-1723

Please include the following information: Parent name, child name, complete address, phone number, sex (M/F), child's birthday, and child's T-shirt size (S, M, L)

(CA and MN residents add applicable sales tax.)

Call toll-free for more information
1-888-FRNDCLB

Kit materials not intended for children under 3 years of age. Kit materials subject to change without notice. Please allow 8-10 weeks for delivery. Offer expires 6/30/99. Offer good while supplies last. Please do not send cash. Void where restricted or prohibited by law. Quantities may be limited. Disney is not liable for correspondence, requests, or orders delayed, illegible, lost or stolen in the mail. Offer valid in the U.S. and Canada only. ©Disney. Based on the "Winnie the Pooh" works, copyright A.A. Milne and E.H. Shepard.

Fun for kids ages 3-8!

Help your child learn MATH and READING with a computer and a silly old bear.

## Disney's Learning Series on CD-ROM

Put your child on the path to success in the 100 Acre Wood, where Pooh and his friends make learning math and reading fun. Disney's Ready for Math with Pooh helps kids learn all the important basics, including patterns, sequencing, counting, and beginning addition & subtraction. In Disney's Ready to Read with Pooh, kids learn all the fundamentals including the alphabet, phonics, and spelling simple words. Filled with engaging activities and rich learning environments, the 100 Acre Wood is a delightful world for your child to explore over and over. Discover the magic of learning with Pooh.

NEW! Disney's Learning Series

Once Again The Magic Of Disney Begins With a Mouse

# Wonderfully Whimsical Ways To Bring Winnie The Pooh Into Your Child's Life.

# Pooh FRIENDSHIP

Pooh and the gang help children learn about liking each other for who they are in 5 charming volumes about what it means to be a friend.

# Pooh STORYBOOK
C L A S S I C S

# Pooh PLAYTIME

# Pooh LEARNING

These 4 enchanting volumes let you share the original A.A. Milne stories – first shown in theaters – you so fondly remember from your own childhood.

Children can't help but play and pretend with Pooh and his friends in 5 playful volumes that celebrate the joys of being young.

Pooh and his pals help children discover sharing and caring in 5 loving volumes about growing up.

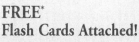

**FREE***
**Flash Cards Attached!**
A Different Set With Each
*Pooh Learning* Video!
* With purchase, while supplies last.